CORK & FUZZ
Merry Merry Holly Holly

by Dori Chaconas illustrated by Lisa McCue

VIKING
An Imprint of Penguin Group (USA)

VIKING
Published by the Penguin Group
Penguin Group (USA) LLC
375 Hudson Street
New York, New York 10014

USA * Canada * UK * Ireland * Australia
New Zealand * India * South Africa * China

penguin.com
A Penguin Random House Company

First published in the United States of America by Viking,
an imprint of Penguin Young Readers Group, 2015

Text copyright © 2015 by Dori Chaconas
Illustrations copyright © 2015 by Lisa McCue

LIBRARY OF CONGRESS CATALOGING-IN-PUBLICATION DATA
Chaconas, Dori, date–
Merry merry holly holly / by Dori Chaconas ; illustrations by Lisa McCue.
pages cm. — (Cork & Fuzz)
Summary: Cork and Fuzz wake up knowing the day is special but not why, and when they
finally find a quiet place to think about it, singing a festive song as a bell jingles and snow
falls on a sparkling pine tree, they realize that their friendship makes every day special.
ISBN 978-0-451-47501-5 (hardback)
[1. Opossums—Fiction. 2. Muskrat—Fiction. 3. Best friends—Fiction. 4. Friendship—
Fiction. 5. Christmas—Fiction.] I. McCue, Lisa, illustrator. II. Title.
PZ7.C342Mer 2015
[E]—dc23   2014049425

Manufactured in China

10   9   8   7   6   5   4   3   2   1

Designed by Jim Hoover

For Mike and Athena, with love.
 —D.C.

To Eileen and Laurie,
Being together makes a day special.
We don't know why, but we can feel it.
 —L.M.

Cork was a short muskrat.

He liked to think. He liked to think about what he might do each day. He liked to think about flowers, birds, snow, and other beautiful things.

Fuzz was a tall possum.

He didn't think about his day. He just followed his nose to wherever it led. He did not think about flowers or birds or snow. He just saw them and said "Ooh!" or "Ahh!"

Two best friends.

One had a head full of thoughts.

The other one seemed to have a head full of air.

"There's something special about today,"
Cork said one chilly morning. "I can feel it."

"Is it your birthday?" asked Fuzz.

"No," said Cork.

"Is it *my* birthday?"

"I don't know what it is," Cork said. "I just feel it. But if we think
really hard, maybe we can figure out why today is so special."

Fuzz groaned. "Thinking hurts my brain," he said.

"When I was little," Cork said, "my grandpa used to say, 'When you need to think, find a good tree to lie under for a little piece of quiet.'"

"When I was little," Fuzz said, "my grandpa used to hook my tail on a branch. He always said, 'Just hang there and think about your behavior.'"

Cork and Fuzz found a large maple tree.

"There's a good tree!" Fuzz said. "We can look up at the leaves while we think."

"There are no leaves," Cork said. "It's winter."

"Then we can watch the tweeters."

Tweek! Tweek! Cheep! Cheep!

"The tweeters sure make a lot of noise," Cork said.

Tweek! Chirp! Cheep, cheep, cheep! Chirp!

Fuzz started to sing along.

"Merry, merry, holly, holly, ho-ho-ho!"

"What kind of song is that?" Cork asked.

"It just came into my head," Fuzz said. "A special day
should have a special song."

Cheep! Cheep! Chirp! Chirp! Tweek! Tweek!

"Merry, merry, holly, holly, ho-ho-ho!"

"I can't think at all with this noise!" Cork said.

"There's no piece of quiet here!"

They crossed over a field to a road, looking for a better tree. A good thinking tree with no tweeters.

"Have you figured out why
this day is special?" Fuzz asked.
"Not yet," Cork said.

"Hey, look what I found!" Fuzz said. "A shiny round stone for my stone collection!"

Jingle! Jingle! Jingle!
"It sings!"

Jingle! Jingle! Jingle!

"Merry, merry, holly, holly, ho-ho-ho!"

"Oh, nuts!" said Cork.

They settled under a branchy oak tree.

"No tweeters," Cork said.

"Only squirtles," Fuzz said.

"Squirtles don't make noise," Cork said.

"This will be a good place for a piece of quiet.
This will be a good place to think."

A squirrel threw an acorn.

Plock!

More squirrels threw acorns.

Plock! Plock! Plock!

Jingle! Jingle! Jingle!
Plock! Plock! Plock!

"Merry, merry, holly, holly, ho-ho-ho!"

"Oh, nuts!" Cork said. "We have to find
a tree with no tweeters and no squirtles."

They found a skinny tree with three skinny branches.

"Cork, it's starting to snow," Fuzz said.

"Shh. I'm thinking," Cork said.

"Cork, it's snowing harder."

"I'm *thinking*."

"If we stay here any longer we're going to be covered in snow," Fuzz said.

"Oh, nuts!"

They walked through the darkening evening
until they found a pine tree. A tree with no birds.
A tree with no squirrels. But a tree that twinkled
with lights.

"A tree with sparkles!" Fuzz said.

They crawled under the tree and looked up
through the glittering branches. Snow fell softly
and silently and even Fuzz's bell was still.

Cork sighed. "A perfect piece of quiet," he said.

"Are you thinking?" Fuzz asked in a whisper.

"Yes," answered Cork. "And I think I've found out why today is special."

"Why?" Fuzz asked.

Cork looked up through the twinkling tree.

"Because I'm in a beautiful place with my friend," he said.

That thought didn't hurt Fuzz's brain at all.

"Yes, yes, yes!" he said. "Being together makes a day special.
We don't know why, but we can feel it."

Fuzz hung the bell on a branch.

It swayed and whispered a gentle song.

Jingle! Jingle! Jingle!

And together they quietly sang,
"Merry, merry, holly, holly, ho-ho-ho!"